I05711179

Wraith Ladies Who Lunch

Wraith Ladies Who Lunch

a weird little thing by

Sean Patrick Traver

RSB

Los Angeles

COPYRIGHT NOTICE

This is a work of fiction. Names, characters, places, and incidents are products of the author's imagination or are used fictitiously. Any resemblance to actual events, locales, or persons, living or dead, is entirely coincidental. This book may not be reproduced in any form, in whole or in part, without express permission from the publisher/copyright holder, except in the case of brief quotations embodied in articles or reviews.

—

Copyright © 2017 by Sean Patrick Traver
Rocket Surgery Books
First Edition / All Rights Reserved.

—

Quote from 'Chuck Palahniuk Answers Your Questions About Everything But His Books,' AV Club interview, used with permission. avclub.com

—

Cover illustration by Amanda Candler amandacandler.blogspot.com

—

www.seanpatricktraver.com

"If you knew that your life was merely a phase or short, short segment of your entire existence, how would you live? Knowing nothing 'real' was at risk, what would you do? You'd live a gigantic, bold, fun, dazzling life. You know you would. That's what the ghosts want us to do — all the exciting things they no longer can."

—Chuck Palahniuk

One

THE LADY TASENETNETHOR, former sistrum player of
Amun-Re, had met Christabel for lunch at the
Cheesecake Factory on every equinox and solstice since
the earliest years of the 21st century.

The restaurant sat several blocks north of her
museum, which was convenient, as Tasenetnethor had to
muster deep earth energies if she meant to send out
further from her preserved remains than a living woman
might comfortably stroll. It was *possible* to project
herself further (the requisite chthonic currents were
eternally churning and available beneath the famous La
Brea Tar Pits, located right next to the lady's latest
resting place at LACMA), but sticking close to home left
her free to spend her strength on being seen. Which was
almost the entire point of her quarterly rendezvous with
Christabel. It wasn't like the ghosts could really eat any

of the treats they ordered, though it did amuse them both to touch the taste buds of the more corporeal diners around them, and pretend.

Vicarious pleasures were better than none at all. Tasenetnethor had reached that conclusion centuries ago. And there were many pleasures to be sought within a few miles of her museum.

For example: the restaurant where she met with her young protégé was part of a majestic shopping complex called The Grove, a place where droves of the city's privileged pretties came to drape themselves in luscious clothes. Next to the mall stood the labyrinthine CBS television studio, where pantomimes and gaming competitions were enacted for broadcast to every known corner of the world. Tasenetnethor loved to haunt the complex's bright stages and its bustling corridors. She'd once been something of a performer herself, as a songstress of the great god, and she felt a certain kinship with show people. She liked being close to them, even if they rarely knew she was there. Watching their acts and studying the near-magical technologies used to disseminate them made her long to participate in their elaborate play, though all she could do was observe. So observe she did. As often as she desired she sat in on theatrical endeavors, catching new movies at The Grove's monstrous multiplex or else taking in avant-garde and classic films at the Cinefamily or the New Beverly, with no need to ever purchase a ticket.

She had no need to ever purchase anything, really.

She had no needs of any kind, at all.

And yet she persisted, now almost three thousand years past the date of her physical demise.

Eternity wasn't all about ennui, however. Her newest tomb—otherwise known as the Los Angeles County Museum of Art—housed more treasures than any royal crypt ever had. Its halls were hers to wander alone by night, unsuspected and unseen. Its vaults were hers to plunder.

While by day she was on public display, snug in her coffin and safe under glass at the center of the hushed Egyptian gallery, where she'd lain in silent repose since 1974.

No stranger to vanity, Tasenetnethor prided herself on being the one piece in LACMA's collection that every schoolkid on a field trip yearned to glimpse—a genuine Theban mummy of the 22nd dynasty. Real human bones wrapped in painted cartonnage, with her transliterated name and a curt description printed on a square of cardstock that sat beside her head and served as her only epitaph.

Few museum patrons guessed that even as they stared at her, she also would examine them. And she found them fascinating. The brief decades she'd spent in this infant city had already proved more stimulating than all of the stultifying, sunbaked centuries that had followed her initial burial, back when the sporadic intrusions of grave robbers had been the only diversion she could hope for.

These days, she more than reciprocated the wonder her contemporary visitors felt when they paused to imagine the details of a long-dead lady's vanished life and times.

But communing with the living was no easy feat, however much she might wish to reach out. They were resistant in so many ways, and she'd learned by painful trial and error that her attempts to connect were more likely to result in madness and heartbreak than anything else. As attractive as she often found modern people, it was better for everyone if she admired the odd novelties of their speech and appearance for a moment or two, then let them get on with their lives.

Wraith Ladies Who Lunch

The museum did contain a number of other ghosts (same as every museum she'd been in), but none of them were quite like Tasenetnethor. The phantoms attached to favored paintings and beloved bits of finery tended to be mere emotional echoes, revenants with no more awareness of the changing times than a recorded voice played back from a vinyl disc might have. Consciousness and will were apparently rather rare amongst the spectral set. The reasons why she and Christabel continued to possess such qualities when others shed them within days of their deaths had been the subject of much debate between them, and together they'd reached some interesting conclusions.

Only a dozen years had passed since the ghost women first discovered one another. By a stroke of luck their easy ranges overlapped like the circles of a Venn diagram, with Christabel hailing from a shop on Melrose Avenue called Necromance, which sold taxidermy and funerary antiques to the morbidly inclined. One autumnal evening when they both happened to be hovering around Pink's hot dog stand at Melrose and La Brea, basking in the restaurant's redolent billows of steam, the pair of ethereal strangers had been shocked to learn that they could not only see each other, but converse as well.

It turned out they had a few things in common, despite a gap of more than two and a half millennia between their ages.

Since that time they'd been meeting up at the turn of each season, if not a little more often. There was nothing stopping them from getting together as frequently as they desired, though after so many solitary decades (time enough for Tasenetnethor to have lost her mind more than once and pieced it back together again), even four meetings in a year felt like a dizzyingly full social calendar. She didn't want to overwhelm her new acquaintance. Besides, she figured they'd have an aeon to socialize, seeing as how it was just the two of their kind sharing the neighborhood.

But that notion only lasted until the equinoctial afternoon when Christabel turned up at their regular Cheesecake Factory table in the company of somebody new.

Two

TASENETNETHOR TRIED NOT TO look taken aback. It wouldn't do to stand there by the hostess station and gape like some sort of antediluvian yokel. Not when Christabel had already seen her, was already on her feet and striding across the sun-splashed entryway to take her hands and kiss both of her cheeks by way of effusive greeting. The older ghost beamed and trilled and returned the gesture, feigning poise since she now had no chance to retreat and reconsider her approach to this unanticipated situation.

Heads turned to follow them. Despite their real ages the women appeared as a pair of effulgent beauties polished to a high gloss, even by LA standards. Christabel presented as an ideal English rose, with her china eyes and poreless porcelain complexion; while Tasenetnethor was a Nile lotus, her almond eyes enormous and her long bronze legs well complemented by a form-fitting linen skirt.

When they made the effort to be seen, they liked to put on a show. And why not? They could appear in any way they remembered from the mortal portions of their experience, and therefore gravitated back to what they felt were their finest hours. Tasenetnethor had been prideful of her hair in life, which was naturally as voluminous as other women's wigs, and today she'd made it look as bountiful as it ever had: a massive mane of springy fronds that fell to the width of her shoulders on its way to the middle of her back. Christabel had been similarly liberal with her own display of cornsilk tresses. The women were nothing more than graceful images in the eyes of their beholders (pictures applied right to those admirers' retinas, in fact, less substantial even than actors on a screen), but that was the game they came here to play.

Tasenetnethor shot suspicious glances past her Dickensian friend's ears as she pecked at each of her spectral cheeks.

The new arrival caught her at it and raised a phantom champagne flute, taunting her with an insouciant grin.

"You're looking vivacious," she said to Christabel, ignoring him, determined to maintain her sophistication in the face of what felt increasingly like an ambush. The compliment was almost a joke—deceased for a hundred and thirty years, the former Victorian was anything but full of life, no matter how youthful she contrived to appear.

"Well, it is the first day of spring," the blonde ghost agreed, then laughed and flashed a vision of her bare, leering skull at a busboy who chose that moment to glance in her direction. He dropped the bin he was carrying, causing a discordant racket that made a dozen diners jump. One sarcastically applauded. An irritable middle-aged manager bustled over and crouched down to help reload the spilled dishes while simultaneously scolding his employee in badly accented Spanish. The skinny kid seemed not to hear, but only gawped at Christabel, who blinked back innocently, with a face restored to unremarkability (except for its considerable beauty). The busser shook his head as if to clear it, muttered 'lo siento, lo siento,' to his nonplussed manager, and scrabbled up a last handful of scattered silverware before hurrying back to the kitchen with his shoulders hunched as if he expected to be struck between them.

"And yes, I'll say it, since you're playing coy," the self-satisfied ghoul-girl said, chiding Tasenetnethor with a wag of her finger. "I found a new one."

"I gathered that."

"So come and meet him."

Tasenetnethor didn't make Christabel drag her (because she would have, like an over-eager child keen on demonstrating some new feat to a jaded parent).

The new arrival stood up and took her hand, though no sensation of contact passed between them. He remembered himself as having been quite good looking at some point in his life, if his ghost was anything to judge by. He'd elected to leave a dusting of silver in his dark hair, which suited him, and he wore the blazer he'd manifested across his broad shoulders like a man familiar with the feel of fine clothing. "Derren Gray," he said. "Christabel's told me all about you, Lady Ta- uh, Tasen—"

"Ta-senet-net-hor," the lady so-named enunciated. "It means 'Sister of Neith and Horus,' after the patron deities of Ta-Senet, the city of my birth, along the Nile south of Thebes."

"Astonishing."

"Is it?"

"I was born in Orange County. In Newport Beach, south of Irvine along the 405."

Tasenetnethor smiled. "That's no less astonishing to me."

"Did you see them build the Pyramids?"

"That was centuries before my lifetime."

"So you don't know if aliens lent a hand?"

"If they did, it would surprise me more than you."

He laughed, though she hadn't meant to say anything funny. He seemed taken with her, perhaps. Christabel was watching them both with a sly look on her deceptively angelic face. Tasenetnethor pushed a stray curl back behind her ear. Despite being witnessed by Christabel on a regular basis, she'd grown unaccustomed to being looked at in the particular way that Derren Gray was looking at her now—though she remembered it with a pang of ancient longing. She wasn't sure this was something she wanted to feel, as there was so little that could be done about it. She wished Christabel would have given her some warning. Being viewed from afar as part of a vernal tableaux was one thing, being seen as one of a pair of pretty women who were meeting for lunch to celebrate the changing angle of the sun's ecliptic, but a triangle of up-close social intercourse was more than she felt prepared to contend with. She reached out with her mind and touched the nervous system of a nearby patron who was deep into her second mojito, hoping the soft-focus warmth she absorbed by proxy might do something to help settle her ambivalence.

"So where did you two find each other?" she asked, claiming a seat at the high-top table they'd staked out before she arrived.

Derren Gray and Christabel laughed together, as if her question had reminded them of a private joke. (And how long had this relationship been established, Tasenetnethor had to wonder, with an unwelcome jab of envy, that they already shared private jokes?)

"It was at Canter's after last orders at the bars, last Saturday night," Christabel said, referring to the classic Jewish deli on Fairfax that turned into a haunt for hungry musicians and glaze-eyed club kids in the small hours. It was the only restaurant in the area to stay open around the clock, and therefore drew all types. Tasenetnethor had been, many times. She liked the smell of the chicken soup, and the creased faces of the oldest servers, who would take rabbis and rock stars in the same shuffling stride. "Caught him loitering in the ladies' water closet," Christabel explained, drifting into the laconic Cockney diction she'd grown up with. "He was takin' the piss with some poor model who'd swallowed so much molly she could almost see him making faces over her shoulder in the mirror."

"It was the first time I'd been seen at all in six months." He offered only a sheepish shrug in defense of his transgression. "Since I... well, you know. I was trying to learn the trick."

Tasenetnethor nodded. She'd been a ghost for so long that she'd almost forgotten about the learning curve, but in truth she hadn't died knowing everything, either. There'd been those terrifying, disconnected years before she figured out she could infiltrate the minds of the living, not only to sample what they felt, but also to make her presence known. "You've made remarkable progress since," she said, taking note of a smartly-dressed businesswoman at a far table who kept casting glances in Derren Gray's direction.

"Thanks to our mutual friend. Christabel here makes a first-rate teacher."

The great educator cocked her blonde head and grinned, making her acceptance of the compliment obvious.

"Your remains must be located nearby."

That remark stalled the conversation more effectively than an unmuffled fart. Christabel pretended to sip her champagne as a pretext for concealing a smirk. Gray chuckled uncomfortably.

"Ah, well, yeah," he said. "At my house, on Gardener, over near the park. Just a few blocks away."

"Cremated? Ashes in an urn? Or scattered?" Tasenetnethor pressed. She realized she was being uncouth, according to the dictates of some modern American phobia regarding funerary customs that she did not share, but now her interest was piqued.

"Cremated, yeah," Derren Gray said, frowning. "Sort of, anyway. Mostly."

"Cremated ghosts usually dissipate even faster than cemetery burials," Tasenetnethor said, considering him anew. "You're an unusual specimen."

"In more ways than one," Christabel agreed.

"Chris explained to me how all of this works. Or how you two have come to think it works. I guess there isn't a vast body of scientific literature on the subject, is there? No standard volumes to consult."

"There's mythological literature," Tasenetnethor said, still marveling that Gray had called the other ghost 'Chris' without getting his head bitten off. "From every culture that has ever been, but none that I've read seems to predict our precise situation. And I've had a great deal of time to read."

"None?"

"Well, there are of course ghost stories. And some cultures have developed ritual methods for avoiding a fate like ours, so the danger is not unsuspected. Vajrayana Buddhists in the Himalayas practice 'sky burial,' where a body is dismembered on a mountaintop and fed to carrion birds in an effort to discourage the escaped 'soul' from identifying with its corporeal remnant, so that it might move on to the bardo realm and later be reborn. But little advice is offered to those who find themselves stuck tight."

She'd turned up nothing helpful in the research libraries at LACMA, anyway; or in the archives of the Museum of Fine Arts, Boston; or in the records of the British Museum before that. Nothing on their giftshop bookshelves, either. Not even the Great Library at

Alexandria (which she'd been able to reach with a concerted and exhausting effort, before it burned) had contained a useful text. And it went without saying that no angel, psychopomp, or other form of ascended being had ever appeared to point the way.

No, every practical thing she and Christabel knew about the afterlife they'd learned through personal observation, the oldest and simplest method of science.

"We thought we had it figured out," Tasenetnethor said, considering. "The thing that separates us from the ghosts that fade, I mean—the trait that Christabel and I share in common. But if you're still here six months after being cremated, our theories may need to be revised."

"That's what I thought too," Christabel said. "But we were right all along. I'm certain of it now."

"Oh?"

"You're talking about the relics, aren't you?" Derren Gray interjected. "The relics and the names? Your mummy at the museum, and Christabel's pendant? The one they have for sale at that creepy antique store?"

Tasenetnethor nodded. Christabel's mourning pendant lay in a display case down the street at Necromance, priced too high to move due to its onyx and platinum construction. About three inches across, the piece contained a woven mat of her blonde hair pressed under glass, framed in black stone, and inset with multiple sapphires that recalled the color of her eyes. Her name was engraved on the back of it, Christabel Anne Thigpen, along with the dates of her birth and death: 1861-1880. Tasenetnethor's name and title were painted in hieroglyphics on her mummy's wrappings, right down the midline of her torso. And that seemed to be the key—those names they couldn't forget.

The original symbol of each individual, a name could serve as an enduring anchor.

"We believe the named relics are what keep us here, yes. But an inscription on an urn or a headstone isn't enough to hold an identity together. Not as far as we've observed. Ghosts packed into graveyards or mausoleums get confused and forget themselves, then either wander as mad revenants or else just disappear. Most people are so traumatized by mortuary practices, decay, or cremation—not to mention the circumstances of their demise—that they dissociate from dead flesh as fast as they can."

"Tell me about it," Derren Gray said with a grimace.

"So how are you here?"

"You're not gonna believe it," Christabel said.

"I might if someone will tell me."

"They made him into a memorial gem!"

"Who did? And what is that?"

"My kids," Derren Gray said.

"It's a diamond," Christabel explained. "An artificial diamond, grown in a lab, cultured from the carbon in his hair and cremated ashes."

"You're joking."

Christabel shook her head. "I've seen it. The stone even has his name and dates laser-etched into one of the facets."

"Engraved on the setting too," Gray contributed.

"Such a thing is possible?"

"Sure," Gray said. "Our bodies are carbon-based, the same element that makes up diamonds. It can be isolated from hair or nails or other tissue. Chemists have been synthesizing diamond crystals from graphitized carbon under high pressure and heat since the 1950s. Several companies offer the memorial service, and some are shadier than others. Thorough cremation destroys a lot of the carbon available in a body, you know—that's kind of what burning is. But assuming enough can be captured, a cultured gem pressed from a unique carbon source? Absolutely possible."

"You know a lot about it," Tasenetnethor observed.

"I've been through it. You pick up a couple of things."

"You weren't a chemist yourself?"

She'd known a chemist once, not so many decades ago. John Thomas Tinsdale, PhD and lifelong fan of historic adventure stories (whose name Christabel always found funny, for some reason), had been contracted to perform a spectrographic analysis on some loose fragments of her wrapping back in 1983. She'd enjoyed the witty facility of his scientific mind, admired his deep understanding of physical reality, and appreciated the romantic, often erotic daydreams about dark-eyed women draped in fragrant linen that his frequent visits to her exhibit had seemed to spark in his imagination. She'd inserted her own image into those fantasies a time or two (or ten), and even tried to confide in him, as her affections began to grow intense. She missed him to this day. Meeting her had not proved to be as much a boon for him, however.

"A chemist?" Derren Gray was saying, in answer to the question she'd almost forgotten asking. "No, no, I was an architect. Well, trained as an architect. Stumbled into real estate development and later into flipping property management companies. Would buy them when they were foundering, retool them, then sell at a profit."

"A lord of land-lords, in the traditional sense," Christabel boasted on his behalf. "Kind of like a king."

Tasenetnethor rolled her eyes, but Gray seemed entertained by the flattery. "Maybe not quite," he demurred, with polite humility. "But I did do pretty well for myself."

A perky young server dressed all in white, who introduced herself as Emily, showed up to take their order. She saw them, through their careful effort, and heard them too, though if anyone happened to review the restaurant's security camera footage later they would see her miming her spiel to an empty high-top table, and nothing more. Between them the women ordered stuffed mushrooms, the chicken samosas, the crispy crab bites, a roasted artichoke, chicken with lemon couscous, and Cajun jambalaya, all dishes being enjoyed at nearby tables. Derren Gray asked for a rare rib-eye steak and a bottle of cabernet sauvignon.

Before her shift was over their server, young Emily, would realize table thirteen had walked out on her. But she would find their plates right where she'd set them, with the food she'd seen them eating untouched and long since gone cold, the whole spread like a spontaneous altar laden with offerings to departed spirits whose names she would never know. The senior staff expected this occurrence by now, four times a year. After closing they would ply an unnerved Emily with drinks and swap stories of the times they'd waited on the wraith ladies themselves.

Tasenetnethor hoped their occasional diversion didn't upset the servers too much. Rattling chains and shouting 'boo' had never amused her, though Christabel, she knew, felt differently. That one had a more natural aptitude for haunting.

"I know it's impolite to ask a lady's age..." Derren Gray ventured, when Emily had flitted off to go put in their extravagant order.

"Hundred and fifty-six, if you count my life," Christabel proclaimed. "Hundred and thirty-seven in this condition."

Gray nodded, apparently imagining the span between then and now. Christabel had been born in London in 1861, the year Victoria's Albert died. Born into a world of mourning, of black crepe and crinoline. Tasenetnethor remembered it well. Egyptology had been a major fad in Europe back then, and she'd spent some time on display in London, at an attraction called the Crystal Palace, after being unearthed outside of Luxor by a Scottish explorer named Robert Hay around 1830. (It was from the Scot that she first acquired a grasp of English, so the odd 'aye' or 'for fuck's sake' was still apt to crop up in her conversation.) Later she would be sold on to a collector in Boston, whose son would donate her to that city's Museum of Fine Arts in 1872. A hundred years after that she was spruced up by conservators and packed off to Los Angeles, as part of a long-term loan of antiquities.

"I was born during the reign of Sheshonq the First, the Pharaoh known as Shishak in the Bible," Tasenetnethor said, when attention turned to her. "So, about two thousand, nine hundred and sixty years ago now. And I died thirty-five years after that—which makes it two thousand, nine hundred and twenty-five years gone, as of this August."

"I don't think I can really imagine that," Derren Gray said.

"Probably not," Tasenetnethor agreed.

"Do you mind if I ask how?"

"I've never been entirely sure what happened." She hadn't thought about her death in ages, and didn't enjoy reflecting on it, even now. "I... sickened. Suddenly. It was horrible. And even though I was relatively young, by the time the end came, I was grateful for the release."

"Fever did for me," Christabel said. "Sinus infection or something like. Came down with it after getting caught out in a freezing rain, one bloody week before my wedding and a month short of my twentieth birthday. Antibiotics would knock it right out, these days. But back then? Death sentence, full stop."

She'd died shivering hard enough to crack her ribs, her lungs bubbling with mucus and her febrile brain broiled past any hope of recovery, even before the physician called to her bedside pronounced her fate with a sorrowful shake of his top-hatted head. Neither of her lunch companions could avoid catching an echo of her memory, and they shuddered at the same time. Gray symbolically topped up her glass of champagne, appearing to finish off the bottle (though a busser would find it full, open yet untouched, when clearing the table later).

"What about you, Derren?" Tasenetnethor asked, while Christabel sipped her imagined Cristal and borrowed the experience of tipsiness from a nearby imbiber's mind.

"What finally took me out, you mean? Mileage. Wear and tear. Cigarettes and whisky. But I made it to eighty-seven with my wits intact, and if that's not past the finish line, then I don't know where it's drawn. Even if I was huffing straight oxygen just to keep from passing out there in the final stretch."

"Eighty-seven," Tasenetnethor repeated, smiling between Gray and Christabel. "You two are practically contemporaries."

"Hey now," Gray said, and Christabel giggled.

"You *are* looking unusually fit for an octogenarian," she teased (flirting shamelessly, in Tasenetnethor's opinion). "Maybe we should call you Dorian Gray."

"Only there's no picture," the young ghost who'd lived longer than both of the women put together said. "Just that ridiculous gem. Do you know it's forty-five carats? That's the size of the Hope Diamond."

"I imagine it will prove very durable," Tasenetnethor mused. "You'll probably outlast us both."

"Do you think?"

"Yeah," Christabel said. "Isn't diamond just about the hardest stuff there is?"

"As far as I know." Gray looked disconcerted by this direction in the conversation.

"That might last ten million years, then. And that's just a number I'm pullin' outta my bum. Unless somebody what, throws it in a volcano? Hardest stone there is? Could last a hundred million years, without Sam and Frodo comin' along. A billion. How long till they say the sun explodes? Till the end of time as we know it? Something like five billion years on, innit?"

Gray was starting to look genuinely unwell, the name that kept him chained to a rock now serving as an apt description.

"Though I suppose something else might incinerate you before that much time goes by, maybe," Christabel hypothesized. "Like an asteroid impact, or a nuclear war, or—"

"Have you ever wanted out?" Gray blurted, looking from one woman to the other. "Out of this? If you could?"

Tasenetnethor and Christabel exchanged a glance. This was not something they discussed, in part because they saw no practical way to effect it (short of conspiring to burn down the buildings that housed their relics, which may or may not have been achievable). Dwelling on the impossibility of escape from their liminal existence could induce a claustrophobic desperation that Tasenetnethor preferred to avoid, these days, since confronting the issue would never resolve it. She suspected that similar feelings stoked the smoldering resentments she sensed in Christabel—fuel for the spite that could flare out from behind her sly demeanor.

Emily spared them having to answer the question by delivering their first round of appetizers, and Derren Gray's red wine.

"I'm sorry if that was the wrong thing to ask," he said, after Emily had poured them each a glass of cab and moved on. "I can see how it might be a sensitive topic."

"I tried," Tasenetnethor said, and Christabel straightened up. She hadn't shared this story with the younger ghost before. The concern that flashed in Gray's eyes melted her a little bit, reminding her of the tender intimacies between individuals that she missed most of all. It was a shame they couldn't touch each other. (She'd tried before with Christabel, but they'd proved mutually intangible.) "This was long ago, so don't worry. At least two thousand years."

"How?" Christabel demanded.

"A tomb robber. A man from Rome, who found my grave after my first thousand years of this existence. His companions looted the amulets and statuary my long-departed family had left behind for me, but this man,

Quintus Caelius, pried open my coffin and ripped up my cartonnage to find a ruby scarab placed underneath the wrapping, despite his friends' urging to let my body alone. At least the grave robbers tended to leave the bodies, you know—though I suppose the archaeologists believe in their reasons, too. Anyway, I followed them, that band of Roman raiders, back to their camp, and that night I invaded Caelius's dreams."

"You can do that?" Gray looked surprised.

"So can you. You're doing it now, with the serving-girl and everyone else who sees you. No difference."

Gray nodded, though he looked unsure. Christabel was silent, frowning.

"In his dream I told the Roman I was angry over my stolen scarab, though I didn't really give a damn. Well, I suppose I did think it was rude. I told him I would claim the lives of his children and his brothers' children in recompense for his trespasses—unless he went back to destroy my mummy and break the curse."

"You never told me about this." Christabel had folded her arms across her chest.

"Well, it didn't work. Obviously. I haven't thought about it. This was back when I still thought the image was the anchor, the recognizable face and form. It's what the priests and the keepers of the necropolis taught us to believe, when I was alive and a part of the court of Amun, and I still believed it then, even though in a thousand years of waiting Anubis had never weighed my heart against the Feather of Truth, or anything else those priests predicted. I hoped eradicating the image I remembered might set me free—though today I have learned the body can be reduced all the way to graphite before those sympathetic bonds are broken."

"Long as the name's kept close-associated," Christabel said. "Yeah, it looks that way."

"Caelius used a rock to smash my face," Tasenetnethor said, as if the other ghost hadn't spoken. "Ruined my painted mask, shattered my jaw, snapped a couple vertebrae. But it didn't get rid of me. The name on my chest was more important than the condition of my corpse."

(In fact she'd see the 1970s before her bones were covered up again, the damaged cartonnage replaced with fresh mulberry paper by a thoughtful preservationist who also cast a new mask from a bust dated to her same dynasty that was in the collection of the Boston museum. The faux face had an elegant jawline and a delicate wedge of a nose, with five damaged fragments of her original portrait recovered from the bottom of her coffin and reassembled jigsaw-style on top of it. Tasenetnethor still appreciated the efforts her conservators had made, and regretted her misadventure with Quintus Caelius.)

"What happened to whatsisname?" Derren Gray asked. "Your Roman?"

"He ran mad into the desert with no water or food, and died in less than two days. I may have frightened him into oblivion by being there when he shed his flesh, because he vanished almost instantly. And I learned that sensing our presence isn't especially beneficial for the living."

"Is our impact always so... detrimental?"

"Not quite so much, not if we're careful. I wasn't careful with Caelius at all. But it's rarely positive, and always a delicate business. Safest for them if they never realize we're anything more than ordinary, if they see us, or else believe we're figments of their fantasies and dreams. Though the kindest thing we can ever do is just to leave them alone."

Christabel harrumphed softly. Gray raised his eyebrows.

"What? Girl's gotta do something for fun," she said, shrugging. "Right? And we've got no power to hurt them, outside of trickery."

"Like you didn't hurt Harry Shelby?"

Tasenetnethor fixed Christabel with a challenging look.

"That's my own private business, what I shared with you in confidence." Christabel's blue eyes narrowed to slits. She looked like a pale snake considering a strike. "No less so 'cause there was nobody else to tell."

"Who's Harry Shelby?" Gray was already attuned to the tension between them.

"Third-rate poet, first-rate tit," Christabel said. "My fiancée, circa 1879. He's the one who had that stupid pendant made, soon as I was in the ground. Clipped the hair in it himself, right off my head in my casket. Wore that awful thing around his neck every day until he drowned, ten years later."

"Which had nothing to do with trickery."

Christabel glared. "And so what if it did? So what if I made him see me underwater, reaching up towards him out of the Strait of Gibraltar while he was spewing cheap wine over the rail of his boat? Honestly. Harry Shelby seized on mourning me as an excuse to shrivel his liver with drink in record time, and he played off the sympathy he received to shag half the whores in Europe while doing it. Good portion of Morocco too. That fucker was lucky I drowned him when I did—probably spared him the trauma of watching his pox-rotted cock drop off!"

"Jesus," Derren Gray said.

"Haven't seen him." An angry Christabel glowered and sniffed. She wouldn't make eye contact. They'd hit a sore spot with her. Their server Emily veered away rather than checking on them, clocking the mood at the table from halfway across the room.

"I never got to do that, not even once," Christabel said, in a more conciliatory tone, after a moment of awkward silence. "And I wanted to. Right? Really wanted to. It's the only reason I agreed to marry Harry Shelby—his curly hair and his stupid dirty poetry that got me all... excited. I figured he'd be really good at it. But I barely knew what 'it' was. Those times, they weren't like today. Nobody talked about anything. Nobody explained. I was only out in that rain in the first place because I'd snuck away to meet Harry in the churchyard, where we could snog and paw at one another behind a headstone for a few minutes before being missed. I was mad to be married, if it meant doing more than that. Now I wish we'd done it sooner.

Done it every chance we got. Wish I'd done it with anybody who looked in my direction, the way heartbroken Harry Shelby got to do, what with his sad eyes and his rotten fiancée. Almost can't even blame him, the miserable shit. His poetry was his real tragedy. Wasn't gonna part a lot of legs on its own merits. He might've killed me on purpose if he'd known how laid a dead girlfriend was gonna get him. And if I'd known I'd be feeding worms in that churchyard myself by the age of twenty, I swear I'd have skipped Harry Shelby altogether and run away to sign on with the nearest brothel before my fifteenth birthday."

Neither of them knew what to say to that. Tasenetnethor had certainly known lovers. Several of them, including her dear Amenemopet, a temple scribe with dexterous hands and a gentle disposition. (She'd be lonely now, tonight, having remembered Amenemopet; his easy smile, his numerous talents. She tried not to do that to herself.) And Derren Gray had said he'd fathered children. They hadn't missed out on the same things as Christabel. They couldn't know her frustrations. Tasenetnethor felt guilty about needling her.

"You can speak now," Christabel said, after a food runner dispatched by Emily dropped off the jambalaya, couscous chicken, and Derren Gray's rib-eye. "I yield the floor."

"I think I read something by a Harold Shelby back in school," Gray said. "One of the minor post-Romantic poets, right?"

"In every sense."

"'The Crystal Bell,' was that about you? About the guy whose lady fair dies of scarlet fever after he accidentally breaks the glass dome she keeps over a magic red rose and it withers?"

Christabel executed a sardonic little bow.

"My sophomore year English teacher loved that poem. My aunt Sheila too. They'd get all weepy about it."

"Too bad Harry wasn't around to buy 'em a drink."

Gray grinned. "You're practically a celebrity. Like the Mona Lisa or Shakespeare's Dark Lady."

That seemed to cheer Christabel a bit. "Do you remember Rhuby Rhude? From the 80s?"

"That depressing singer with the bright red hair and all that black lace? My daughters used to listen to her, I think. My older two, the twins, Rachel and Gwen."

"Yeah, that's her, the 'post-punk postmodern goth-style icon,' according to her autobiography. Rhuby loved that poem so much she bought the mourning pendant one of Harry Shelby's friends snatched from his funeral pyre on the beach where his body washed ashore, when it went up for auction at Sotheby's. In the 90s she found heroin, then Jesus. But in between she paused to sell me off to Necromance."

"Used to wonder if their mother should have the girls on suicide watch when they were into that stuff. Pentagrams, Ouija boards, Tarot cards—they embraced every cliché. Always figured they did it mostly to piss me off. Worked pretty well, if that was the plan."

"I suppose that was my attempt, when I upset Harry's balance and knocked him in the drink. If we're doing true confessions." A thoughtful Christabel looked across the table at Tasenetnethor, who had difficulty not looking away. "Figured I'd been haunting *him* all that time. Didn't understand about the pendant, not then. Thought if he shuffled off, we could go our separate ways. Which I guess is pretty much what happened, only he went, and I stayed."

Tasenetnethor nodded. She had little right to judge, as her own behavior had not always been above reproach. Quintus Caelius was not the only mortal she'd ever injured. She might've patted the younger ghost's hand or something by way of apology, maybe even hugged her, but in this case she thought the pantomime would feel empty and unsatisfying. Not to mention awkward. Any pretense of physical contact between them was strictly a show for the incarnate rubes around them, a part of playing at vitality. "I... regret what I said."

"S'all right. No harm done." The blonde flashed her wicked smile. "'Cept of course to Harry Shelby."

"And to the annals of English verse," Derren Gray said, causing Christabel to snort.

"I'm surprised you let him get away with philandering in your name for as long as ten years, when I think of it like that." Tasenetnethor took a sip of imaginary wine.

"Eh, well, I might not've ever figured out my trick, without such ample inspiration. Envy can bring your creative side right out, that's for certain."

"I assume she has demonstrated this for you?"

"The sex thing, you mean?"

"That's a nice description of an innovation this one never twigged to, not in three thousand years."

"Twenty-nine hundred," Tasenetnethor said, feeling miffed at having her millennial lack of ingenuity pointed out. "And change."

"Your Vulcan mind-meld with couples, then." Gray's eyes crinkled with amusement. "Your magic mental mound-meld."

"It is a good trick." Tasenetnethor wasn't going to hector her any further about endangering the living people she involved in her games (especially since this was a game she now played herself, though not with Christabel's avidity).

Sometime in the 1920s, in Berlin, after having been passed down by a couple of collectors as an invisible addendum to the mourning pendant once commissioned by the late poet Harold Shelby, it had occurred to Christabel to touch both minds of a couple locked in the throes of passion at the same time. The first result of this maneuver, more often than not, was a simultaneous climax for the fortunate fuckers, as the dead Victorian virgin became a bridge between them and experienced the totality of their performance from dual perspectives. It tended to delight the couple (and that tradeoff was what allowed Tasenetnethor to rationalize her own creepy, uninvited participation in living strangers sex lives), but it could also open them to each other in nonstandard ways. Unexpressed needs, undiscussed fetishes, and unwelcome ideas could all breach the normally inviolable barrier of individual consciousness in that moment of harmonic convergence, with consequences that were not always benign. In some cases too much intimacy too soon smothered nascent affections; in others, significant antipathies burst to the surface with no warning, manifesting in shouting, division, and tears. Close, established partnerships tolerated their presence best, and Tasenetnethor tried to limit her activities to a circle of stable yet playful regulars who lived close to the museum. But here again Christabel behaved differently. The aspiring succubus craved neoteny, the reiterated thrill of something new, the heat and tension of a fresh infatuation, and would latch onto any likely pair that drew her eye along Melrose or Wilshire. Her incautious approach poisoned plenty of budding relationships that might otherwise have grown and flourished, but about this, Christabel gave not a single shit. If anything she felt she was doing her disillusioned lovers a favor by encouraging them not to waste their fleeting appeal, but rather to exploit it as widely and licentiously as possible.

Tasenetnethor took care to do no (or little) harm, but the prospect of luxuriating in every blissful squish from either side of the sexual equation was too much for a lonely ghost to forego forever. Or for long. She was grateful to Christabel for the new pastime, but, even though the experience often left her more shaken than her host couples themselves, there was still something... *thin* about it. Insubstantial. Like inhaling all the scents of a rich meal but absorbing none of the nourishment, and still feeling hungry when presented with the bill.

Gray seemed to echo her unshared assessment when he said, "Yeah, it's something, I'll grant you. Better than nothing at all ever again, I guess."

"That all?" Christabel looked crestfallen. "Better'n nothing?"

"I mean, the living would envy it, if they knew about it, definitely." Gray seemed to know he'd impugned her discovery, but would only backpedal partway. "But it's still not, you know, the same. Like having a vivid dream. It's great, you wouldn't turn it down, but mostly it just makes you want the real thing more."

"Wouldn't know, would I?" Christabel appeared not only disappointed, but worse, resigned to it. Tasenetnethor had seen the same expression on the faces of potential suicides contemplating the leap from the top of The Grove's multistory parking garage.

Wraith Ladies Who Lunch

The mood at the table had palpably shifted. They all had a lot to think about. None of them were even pretending to eat, despite the plates that crowded their tabletop. The deficiencies of make-believe were too much on their minds. They looked—and felt—like they were starting to sober up after a couple rounds of drinks.

"They... couldn't have known what they were doing, could they?" Derren Gray asked, almost rhetorically, appearing deeply troubled by the idea. "My kids? Consigning me to this?"

"Wondered that myself, regarding Harry," Christabel said, scowling into her wine glass. "He told everyone who remarked that he wore that ugly pendant to keep me close forever. And he always was one for séances and spiritualists and all that brand of crap. Though look who's talking now."

Her bitter bark of laughter turned heads at the next table.

"Was one of his spiritualist twats made my pendant for him, I know that much. Told him to write my name on a ribbon and tie that lock of hair with it when he cut it off. Was that meant to keep my brains and that little piece of my remains stuck together like they are? Maybe. Can't know at this late date, can I? But I could kill that

Harry Shelby all over again, if he did this to me on purpose."

"My lover Amenemopet had a wife before me," Tasenetnethor murmured. It hurt to speak of Amenemopet even now, on a continent and in an era he could never have imagined. "Isetnofret was her name. And she had a brother, Ptahshepses, a priest of the Necropolis. Ptahshepses was a terrifying man, corrupt and often secretly contracted to perform unsanctioned rites of death and vengeance magic. I have sometimes wondered if Isetnofret might not have poisoned me. She was one of those who served spiced wine at the Festival of Drunkenness the year I died, so she might have had a chance. I fell ill that night and never recovered. And it was Ptahshepses who performed my mummification."

"Huh," Christabel grunted. "Was a punter called 'Thom Shepcease' who made Harry's mourning pendant. Sounds almost the same."

"Thom Shepcease?" Derren Gray said. "Thom with a 'th'?"

"That's right."

"But that's the name of the diamond guy. The guy from the company that pressed my diamond for Rachel and Gwen. Gemetic Memories. Founder and CEO. He oversaw the whole process personally. Should have, too—they paid him thirty thousand dollars for that goddam rock."

"How weird," Christabel said. "About the name. What do they call that? Synchronicity, innit?"

"What does it mean?" Derren Gray looked to Tasenetnethor, as the most senior and knowledgeable amongst them.

"I haven't the first idea," she said, although she did. They all did. She could see it in the eyes of the other two.

"Were they all the same person?" Derren Gray said. "Is that in any way possible?"

"No," Tasenetnethor said.

"But is it true?"

"It can't be."

"My Thom Shepcease was a goldsmith who led séances and collected old books," Christabel said. "Peculiar bloke. Tall. Bald. Foreign, but hard to say from where."

"Mine has the old books, all right," Gray said. "A library at the Gemetic Memories lab up near San Francisco that's practically a museum. I was still hovering around when he gave the girls a tour of his collections. He has a First Folio of Shakespeare, from

1623. Did he buy that when it was new? Hot off the Gutenberg press?"

"Nobody doesn't die." Tasenetnethor was adamant. She'd seen a lot in her twenty-nine hundred years (and change), but nothing like that.

"He's got the bald head too. Little beard, good suit. Superior attitude. I think the girls were both sort of attracted to him," Gray said, looking queasy at the memory. "In fact I know they were. That was when I first learned I could walk away from my remains, at least for a couple miles."

Tasenetnethor didn't want to ask what form Gray's middle-aged daughters' mutual attraction to the man who might've been Ptahshepses had taken. Knowing that something he'd seen had prompted him to take his first noncorporeal stroll was enough for her imagination.

"He must be a descendant," she insisted, though the priest's longevity was not the focus of Gray's concern, and he didn't really seem to hear her.

"They cremated my body, but not my viscera," he said. "Stomach, entrails, liver and lungs. Funeral home gave those over to Gemetic Memories, whose techs packed them into Styrofoam coolers with my name written on all four sides, plus the bottoms and the lids. Written on the zip-bags they were wrapped in, too. Along with my hair, which they shaved off, and my nails, ripped out one by one with a pair of pliers. So they could be sure to get a good carbon sample, they said."

Tasenetnethor was thinking he'd named the very organs Ptahshepses of the Necropolis would have sealed into canopic jars when vivisecting a fresh mummy-to-be, but she didn't say anything about it. "The impossibility of not dying aside," she mused instead, "the odds of three victims of his magic who never put that together before meeting by chance centuries later must be astronomical."

"But doesn't havin' all the time in the world mean we'll beat every set of odds, eventually?" Christabel astutely pointed out. "Not about 'if,' is it? Only 'when.' Means there might be others too, ghosts we haven't met yet. World's a big place, and our man's been in it a long time."

Tasenetnethor found she had no further arguments to mount. The notion had a sick certitude to it, despite its wild improbability, and she felt unsettled to think that terrible Ptahshepses had walked the earth since before she even died.

How many others had he condemned to this twilight half-life, in all the years since then? Was his name the key to his longevity as well, its pronunciation (or some reasonable variant) maintained across the centuries? She remembered him as a man of awful appetites and nefarious reputation, prone to rages and vendettas in the face of any perceived form of disrespect. He had a taste for the company of the temple's musicians and dancers, but the women who fell prey to his superficial charm all came back changed, whispering nightmare reports of his depravity. His position and influence ensured they never raised their voices louder. Tasenetnethor had felt his eye on her many times, tracking the shimmy of her hips as she danced during the daily rites held in the forecourt of the Temple of Amun. Every now and then it upset her so badly that she missed a beat with her sistrum, which would leave her feeling humiliated and defensive for the rest of the morning. She'd evaded his attentions the way a hare dodges a circling hawk. Remembering the few unavoidable occasions on which he'd managed to stroke her skin with his natron-leathered fingers still made her shudder with revulsion.

He might very well have been cruel and petty enough to do this to her, especially if Isetnofret, his bitch of a sister, asked it of him. Tasenetnethor had little trouble believing that.

But could Ptahshepses really still be out there now, alive and well and operating some sort of modern-day alchemist's lab up near San Francisco? Calling himself Thom Chesspiece, or whatever it was the others had said? Still refining the nomenclatural necromancy that could hold a soul in bondage for untold thousands of years, while gorging himself on every pleasure the living world had to offer, well beyond any mortal's normal allotment? The idea was abhorrent to her. Maddening.

But that didn't mean it wasn't so.

Even after three thousand years, there were things between heaven and earth she had yet to discover. But, thanks to Ptahshepses, she still had plenty of time.

All three of them had fallen silent, considering the betrayals that had brought them to this place. Christabel's hump-happy poet, and the weird sisters Derren Gray had apparently sired. How had they failed in those relationships so disastrously that people they'd loved had wanted to see them cast out of eternity? Tasenetnethor couldn't know, though maybe she would. Again, it looked like they had plenty of time.

It would appear that her own dire offense had been loving Amenemopet. Of that she was guilty, and unrepentant. Her deepest sorrow was that she hadn't shared a full life with him. Now that her ancient suspicion that she might have been robbed of it had concretized into a stark new certainty, she was at a loss for how to feel. Though angry seemed like a pretty fine choice, as she reviewed her options.

What she might possibly do about that anger was another matter.

Tasenetnethor looked at her companions. Christabel was toying with the hem of the knee-length caftan she'd come dressed in, reminiscent of the fashions from the 1960s and 70s and no doubt copied from a store window somewhere here at the mall, same as her own silk top and linen pencil skirt. The long-dead Lolita harbored such nostalgia for the hedonistic abandon of her favorite bygone times. Tasenetnethor didn't blame her. She supposed she'd never get past her own affinity for linen, or her fondness for black eyeliner.

Derren Gray, for his part, seemed to have aged ten years in the last ten minutes. His spectral projection was withering as his attention turned inward, without enough psychic focus allocated to keep the illusion going. His hair, tinged with silver less than an hour ago, was halfway white already. His faraway eyes were still retreating into deepening nests of wrinkles.

Wraith Ladies Who Lunch

Today's salon, meant only to mark the turning of the earth and the warming of the weather, had proved more illuminating than any of them expected. The revelations they'd uncovered seemed to have damaged the youngest amongst them.

"It seems we've all found much to consider," Tasenetnethor said, tipping her head toward Gray, whose time-lapse decline was sure to startle someone living at any moment. He looked like he'd been re-cast late in their production's run, with his own father stepping into his role. "But perhaps it is time we were on our way. Until the solstice, then?"

Christabel nodded and nudged Gray with an elbow. He broke from his reverie with a start, straightening his bent spine and pulling a little color back into his hair. He still looked like a disheveled, shellshocked wreck of the ghost who'd walked in and ordered champagne. "Yes, absolutely," he said, attempting to catch up with the conversation (though he couldn't chase that newly haunted look from his eyes). "It was a pleasure to meet you, Tasenetnethor of Thebes."

"You as well, Derren Gray of Orange County."

And the next time Emily passed by their table, she realized all three of them had gone.

Three

ALL TASENETNETHOR HAD to do to return to the museum
was to let go, to quit making the effort that maintained
her projection. As soon as she relaxed she found herself
delivered back to her place of rest—the Egyptian gallery
on the third floor of LACMA's Hammer Building. The
experience was as quick and painless as a cut in a movie.

She spent the late afternoon haunting the crowded
courtyard that was bounded by the Hammer, Ahmanson,
and Art of the Americas buildings, unseen and trying to
peer into peoples' computers.

Both the laptop and the handheld 'phone' style
devices were much in use at the tables scattered between
the museum complex's structures, where gallery-goers
could perch to enjoy a cup of coffee or a sandwich in the
bright spring sun. Computers (the new world's
astonishingly reliable answer to the scrying stones of

classical seers) were an ongoing source of fascination for her, though she found them more difficult to access than books.

Books inherently contained what they contained— even the ephemeral ghost-copies she could pick up and interact with for a while. Such simulacra possessed all the same qualities as the living-world originals, down to printed words on a page. Not so with computers. Information came channeled to them from faraway sources, and simply would not appear according to her will when she pecked at an astral analogue of somebody's borrowed iPhone. The only way she could get at The Internet was to find a device already open to the webpage she wanted. Long odds. Briefly possessing someone in order to use Google might technically have been possible, though not at all easy, and probably traumatic for the commandeered individual.

But she didn't need such extreme measures. A new collection of contemporary jewelry was on display on the plaza level of the Ahmanson, and several inspired viewers of it searched for 'gems' in their black mirrors. Tasenetnethor could cause a living finger to twitch without revealing herself and scaring its owner, enough to register a second 'e' on the keyboard rather than the intended 's,' at which point the search algorithm would offer up 'Gemetic Memories' on a drop-down menu of auto-complete options. After several tries at this, one elderly woman with a recently expired spaniel on her mind felt enough morbid curiosity to click the link, and Tasenetnethor had what she wanted.

She seized a ghostform copy of grandma's Samsung (which went entirely unnoticed by the phone's real owner), clicked the 'About Us' button on the open website's banner, and there he was.

Ptahshepses.

Or at least a digital photograph of him, wearing Armani and posed before a glass-and-steel laboratory building that sat situated atop a distant hill.

Tasenetnethor almost dropped the phone, but caught it in time. (She didn't know if a ghost-copy would break the same as a real one, but she didn't want to start this process over.)

Ptahshepses, or 'Thom Shepcease,' (not *Chesspiece*) was indeed a pioneer in the science of making diamonds out of dead people, up in northern California. His bald pate and long patrician face were unmistakable to her, even after the lifecycle of several empires. The fancy suit did nothing to disguise him.

Wraith Ladies Who Lunch

The Gemetic website had an address for their facility, as well as a map link, which Tasenetnethor selected. She'd never seen San Francisco before, and needed a sense of the territory.

Then she dropped down into the black earth below the museum, which was as permeable to her as any other physical thing. The local Tar Pits (well-plumbed by geo-bio- and paleontologists, seeing as they were layered with the semi-liquid remains of many thousands of years' worth of indigenous beasts, birds, and people) had long been a powerful fount of chthonic force, a geyser of geomantic vigor extruded from deep fissures under immense tectonic pressure.

Tasenetnethor soaked it in as she dove through the bituminous underground darkness, gathering the strength she needed to launch her consciousness on a long arc across a gilded evening sky, aiming north.

Four

SHE MET WITH RAIN ABOVE San Francisco, which didn't make it easy to match the terrain below with the satellite picture she'd looked at on the web. Rain was still something of an exotic novelty to her, even after all her years in Boston and Britain, but she didn't feel like being soothed by its music now. She only wanted to find Ptahshepses. To glimpse him in his unnatural habitat.

Now that she knew there was specific intent behind her condition, she supposed she had read of something that might be considered similar—the *Nganga* of West African sorcerers, an iron cauldron into which human remains were permanently sealed by means of spellwork, concrete, and physical chains. This lurid assemblage was meant to enslave a deceased victim's spirit for an afterlife of earthbound servitude. Tasenetnethor didn't know if she wasn't under Ptahshepses' sway right now because he lacked the power to control her, had forgotten about her, or because he considered her small ability to bear witness too trifling a thing to exploit.

She hoped for the former, but expected one of the latter two options.

In any case, she couldn't find him. The old priest must have hexed up his lair, erected wards to blind spies and disorient intruders. Of course he had—he must have known all the magic of ancient Greece and Rome, not to mention that of the Phoenicians, the Persians, and the Babylonians too. Plus the Picts, the shamans of Siberia, and the unholden of Bohemia, after centuries of nomadic migration. Probably also the psychedelic witches and the chaos mages of the internet, by now. Ptahshepses had always been a careful scholar. He knew what he was doing. Amorphous Tasenetnethor grew dizzy when she neared the lab's hilltop above the city, lost her way, failed to recognize geographical landmarks below. Some imperceptible force of will was deflecting her, and she shouldn't have been surprised. A man who'd survived for three thousand years was certainly one who knew how to hide out in plain sight.

After three exhausting hours she gave up on reconnaissance and let herself snap back to the museum.

And, though closing time had come and gone, she wasn't especially shocked to find Derren Gray waiting by her coffin to see her.

Five

THEY WALKED; he talked.

"What does it mean to pass on, do you think?" he asked, as they wandered the dim corridors of the Ahmanson building. "Further on than this, I mean. The way it goes for most ghosts."

"I suspect your guess is as good as mine."

They found their way into the Indian art gallery—a hall filled with exotic gods, a carved pantheon reduced to multilimbed shadows in the after-hours gloom. Tasenetnethor stopped before her favorite stone Ganesha to rub his polished boulder of a belly for luck, something the museum docents had long allowed visiting schoolchildren to do as well. The sculpture pulsed with temporary memory as a result, a paisley-swirl of earnest, innocent wishes, appreciated only by her.

"Is it just oblivion for the ones who go? Or is there more than this?"

"That's the biggest question there is, Derren Gray."

"Yeah, and what do you think?"

She thought, after all this time, that humanity's catalogue of beliefs on the subject was an atlas packed with maps drawn by half-blind cartographers, attempting to chart an indescribable territory. She summed this up with a shrug. "Some sort of more, I expect. Though maybe only insofar as the environment recycles our molecules. Why do you ask?"

"I failed my children," Derren Gray said. No evasion—owning up. "My girls. I see that now. Real clearly."

Tasenetnethor thought it would be impolite to agree that yes, they sounded awful, so she kept silent.

"I died slow enough to examine my regrets," Gray continued. "I know I wasn't a perfect father. I was never violent, or, you know, as bad as the worst fathers can be, but I was... disapproving. Distant. Disappointed, and disappointing. I can't even say I always liked the girls. They're so much like their mother was, and we didn't like each other for years before we split. But I did love them. I do love them, I mean—death doesn't put an end to that. Even though I never understood them. They were angry, difficult teenagers, and truth be told they're not much different as grown adults. And some of the blame for that belongs on my doorstep. Maybe most of it."

He looked into Ganesha's small, wise eyes.

"I'd started to take comfort in ideas like these, before the end," he said, tipping his chin toward the elephant-headed Lord of Obstacles. "Reincarnation. An afterlife. Something. Even though I'd never had a lot of patience with philosophy. It was my wife's influence, I'm sure. My second wife, Nora. Not the girls' mother. Nora, you know, believes in things. More readily than me. But that idea, that there might be another chance of some sort after death, maybe at least to do a little better next time around if not to really make things right, with practice—that'd started to sound pretty nice. I suppose I was counting on it. But now I know that's more than my girls think I deserve. Even if there's another chance available, in some existence beyond this one, they don't want me to have it. They'd rather just... ditch me. For good. For eternity."

Derren Gray looked unutterably sad, even in the dark. Tasenetnethor was grateful for the veil of night.

"I knew I was far from perfect," he said. "But I didn't know I'd earned that."

Tasenetnethor nodded. Christabel could attribute her entrapment by Harry Shelby more to romantic idiocy than malice, maybe, but the two of them, herself and Derren Gray, they knew that people had hated them. Loathed them enough to want to see them spun right off the rim of Samsara's wheel. But there'd been no love lost in life between Tasenetnethor, her killer Isetnofret, and her preserver Ptahshepses. It still wasn't the same as being condemned and cast out by one's own children.

"I never was a parent, myself..." she said, unsure of what else to say, or what insight he thought she might have. She'd never taken precautions to avoid pregnancy, yet it never occurred. She could only imagine the weight of the blow his daughters' vehement rejection of him had dealt to Gray's psyche. He didn't look as concussed as he had by the end of their lunch, but some part of him was still reeling, and she had to wonder if he would ever see his equilibrium restored.

"I'm not sure I was ever a parent either, in any of the ways that matter. At least to the twins. My youngest was a different story. Cordelia. I think I did a little better with her."

A small, unconscious smile touched the corners of his lips when he said her name. Tasenetnethor could hear it in his tone better than she could see it.

"Different mother. More than ten years apart. Never had a real relationship with her mom, just an affair, and that's what finally broke up my first marriage. The twins hated Cordie for it. They hate their stepmom too, even though it wasn't Nora I cheated with, and I guess that hasn't changed. They gave her that damn diamond I'm tied to, you know. And I actually thought they might be making a genuine peace offering, in their own weird way. But it was only their sick ironic idea of a fucked-up joke."

Gray's frustration was radiant enough for Tasenetnethor to feel.

"What is it you hope I can tell you, Derren?"

"I don't really know. Maybe just how you've managed to face this, day after year after century."

"By not having any other choice."

Derren Gray nodded. Tasenetnethor thought perhaps she'd been too blunt, but there wasn't any better answer, and she'd forgotten how to soften hard truths.

"Well, those TV ads say diamonds are forever, so I guess I'll have time enough to work out some coping mechanisms of my own."

Personally, Tasenetnethor thought 'forever' was a very strong word.

"Can I see it?" she asked. "Your stone?"

Six

GRAY COULD SNAP BACK home, but Tasenetnethor didn't know how to follow if he did, so they strolled, just like a living couple. It didn't take long and the weather was nice, though not even arctic temperatures would have bothered them. The ghosts could detect hot and cold, but were adversely affected by neither condition.

Gray's home turned out to be a mid-20th-century ranch-style affair, with four bedrooms and a swimming pool oasis nestled into a small but leafy back yard. The house, while certainly comfortable, and located in a fashionable neighborhood, was still more modest than she might have expected, given the rumors of Gray's vast wealth.

"It's Nora's now," he said of the single-story bungalow, as he stepped aside to let Tasenetnethor pass through the front door before him. "Really always was.

She chose it and loved it, and I was glad I could give it to her. And now the twins are trying to take it away."

"They are?"

"Contesting my will, at any rate. Even though I divided five million dollars amongst the four of them. Nora, Cordie, Rachel and Gwendolyn. Nora wanted the bulk of the estate to go to various organizations—the ACLU, Doctors Without Borders, even some to your museum—but Rachel and Gwen feel they're entitled to a bigger cut of the pie. If not the entire goddam thing."

"But not your Cordelia?"

"Cordie makes her own money," Derren said. "Her million's for safety. Nora's too. Nora's a ceramicist, you know. Makes art pottery that's shown in galleries all around the world. Keeps her workshop and kiln in the back bedroom. She had a career before she ever knew me. And Cordie's a location manager for movies and TV. She travels and scouts and books places for productions to shoot."

Tasenetnethor found the note of pride in his voice rather endearing. She spotted several pieces of graceful teaware and other abstract porcelain forms on display in the glass-fronted bookcases that lined the living room walls.

"Diamond's back this way." He motioned for her to follow and crept down the hall, as if his inaudible footsteps could disturb anyone's sleep. But habits died harder than the people who kept them.

They found Cordelia herself in the spare bedroom, dozing fully clothed on top of the covers, with the menu from a DVD copy of *Wings of Desire* that had already played to the end sitting open on her laptop computer. Tasenetnethor had watched that film herself, more than once, in the museum's screening room and at the New Bev too.

"She's staying here tonight before they go see the lawyers in the morning, trying to work out the issues with the will," Gray explained. It wasn't late—not yet ten o'clock—and they could hear someone, presumably Nora, shuffling about in her back-room studio.

He picked up a simple wooden box (or a ghost-copy of it) from the dresser and handed it to Tasenetnethor.

Inside she found an obscenely large brilliant-cut diamond with a deep azure tint, set into a sleek, teardrop-shaped silver pendant. The rock was the size of a fat olive, with astonishing depth and clarity. A product of uncontaminated lab conditions, it appeared to have no flaws or inclusions at all. If it had an imperfection it was that it appeared too perfect to be anything other than artificial.

"Look around the girdle," Gray said. "The edge of the stone. Look close."

She did, and there it was, his name, Derren Gray, accompanied by his dates of birth and death, all etched in characters too miniscule for living eyes to read without the aid of a magnifying glass.

"Traces of boron in the ash sample made it blue," he said as Tasenetnethor held it up to the light. "They say the shade varies from person to person. Seems there's individuality left even when we're carbonized."

"Enough, anyway," Tasenetnethor murmured, admiring the stone's hard sparkle.

"I croaked down the road at Cedars, but this is the last room I lived in," Gray said, looking down at his drowsing daughter. Cordelia appeared to be in her late thirties or so (a bit younger than her father's ghost looked now, and a bit older than Tasenetnethor had been at the time of her death). She had auburn hair and good taste in shoes, judging by the pair of low-heeled Louis Vuitton pumps she'd kicked into the corner before flopping down to doze in front of her movie. The footwear had fetched up against a pair of large steel canisters in the corner, each about four feet high. They had handles on their sides and would have resembled old-fashioned milk cans, except for the big plastic valve-caps crowning their tops.

"Liquid O_2 reservoirs," he explained, when he saw Tasenetnethor eyeing them. "To refill my portable oxygen unit from. For hypoxemia. Nora called, but the medical supply place still hasn't come to get those damn things out of here."

He sounded self-conscious, she noticed, even defensive—as if growing old was a personal failing and not a privilege many never knew. "Does it make you uncomfortable to be in here?"

"A bit. Yeah. I guess it does."

Tasenetnethor tipped her head toward the open door, then preceded him into the hallway when he nodded in agreement.

She couldn't help but look into Nora's well-lit studio, one door down the hall. The room was large, with a slanted wood-beam ceiling, white walls, a clay-caked worktable, a potter's wheel in the corner, and wire racks lined with jars of colorful liquid glazes. A sliding glass door at the rear of the room opened onto a covered patio, where an ethereal yet earthy woman in perhaps her mid-sixties, presumably the Widow Gray, was checking the pyrometric cones inside an electric kiln stationed by the wide doorway. She had her silver-shot blonde hair drawn back into a loose ponytail, and wore a pigment-spattered sweatshirt with frayed old jeans. The kiln she was firing seethed with an intense heat that glowed through at the boxy device's seams.

"She always liked to work at night," Derren Gray said in a deferential murmur (as if that were necessary). "Cooler in the spring and summer. Little more cost-effective to heat up that beast during off-peak hours, too."

"She makes lovely things."

Gray nodded, both agreeing and accepting the compliment on Nora's behalf. "I was selfishly glad I wouldn't have to watch her die, you know. Her and Cordie both. Feels a bit like hubris now."

Tasenetnethor had no comforting response. He was right. He would not only have to watch his loved ones wither and suffer and die but, thanks to Ptahshepses, he'd also get to remember it forever.

"It seems like you had good relationships with them."

"Yeah, now I do. Did, by the time I died. Nora wasn't the mother of any of my kids, but she helped me deal with regrets I'd only been denying, and I had time to make things better. With Cordelia, at least. The twins, they're another story."

Tasenetnethor felt her next logical question (*what went wrong there?*) was one she could leave unspoken.

And Gray shrugged, picking up on her silent implication. "Their mother and I, I'm not sure we ever loved each other, really, so much as... wanted what we each thought the other represented. You know what I mean? In any case it ended badly, with affairs and accusations and lots of yelling. Rachel and Gwen were just old enough to understand everything. And they've always blamed Cordelia for it. Going after the estate's more about vindictiveness than any need of the money."

"What do you think will happen?"

"Well, nobody's looking forward to this meeting tomorrow. Twins have some high-powered lawyers in their pockets. They've both been married more than once, and they made out all right on settlements. God knows their mother and I didn't set them any great example in that arena. So it's gonna be a fight. Probably an ugly one. And this has been hard on Nora and Cordie already. Hurtful. Difficult to watch. The twins can be so... well, whatever. I just wish there was something I could do."

"Do you really think they'll lose?"

"Who? Nora and Cordie? Oh, hell no. The twins have some crackerjack lawyers, but mine's a piranha in a suit. That will is ironclad. Nora and Cordelia are fine, and they'd be fine even if they did happen to lose tomorrow. I have faith in them. It's the twins whose lives have been so full of, of... venom, and recrimination. Poison that they spread around. They've been so unhappy. I'd help that, more than anything. But I'd need another lifetime to do it in."

Tasenetnethor nodded, having quietly decided to offer her assistance.

"Would you go, if you could, Derren Gray? On the off chance?"

"The off chance of reincarnation?"

"Or something like it. Something more."

"Nora likes ideas like that." Gray watched his widow as she fiddled with her equipment. "We talked about them a lot. Transmigration, she called it, and soul-clusters too. Entities whose fates are entwined across time, who might swap relationships back and forth over many multiple incarnations. I'm not as sure about that stuff myself, even now. Seems a pretty long shot that I might meet the girls again and do better by them in some life that's yet to come."

"But would you gamble on it?"

Derren Gray looked her in the eye. "I would, if I could. Yes. I would. Now what aren't you telling me? Is there some way to make that happen?"

"Maybe," Tasenetnethor said. "For you, there might be. Would you like to try?"

Seven

"WOULDN'T WE HAVE TO destroy the diamond? Or at least get my name off it?"

Tasenetnethor shrugged. "They aren't really forever. Commercials tell lies."

She led him back into the guest room currently occupied by Cordelia Gray. Her rest was shallow, her thoughts an uneasy mix of dream and reflection. Tasenetnethor spotted the discarded wrapper from a medicinal cannabis brownie lying in the wastepaper basket beside the bed.

"Nora gave that to her. They helped me sleep, before the end. And Cordie's stressed about tomorrow," Gray explained, perhaps inferring a criticism Tasenetnethor did not intend. She was glad Cordelia had eaten the brownie. Its psychoactive effects would make her unexpected presence in the living woman's mind feel far less obtrusive.

She sat down on the edge of the bed and looked up at Derren Gray. "I'm going to give her an idea."

"Please be careful," he said, looking concerned. "Please don't hurt her."

Tasenetnethor shook her head. "I'll be as gentle as a whisper."

Gray reluctantly nodded his assent.

Tasenetnethor stroked Cordelia's reddish hair, merged into the flow of her cognition, and let herself remember a demonstration she'd once watched John Thomas Tinsdale perform before an auditorium packed with UCLA chemistry students, back in the middle of the 1980s.

Cordelia snapped awake with a start. Tasenetnethor stood up and stepped back, to stand beside an anxious Derren.

The youngest of the sisters Gray sat up, yawned, shook out her hair and pinned it back with a plastic clip. She frowned, glancing over at the diamond pendant in its box on the shelf, then pulled her laptop close.

The ghosts crowded in to watch her type the words 'burning a diamond' into a Google search field. The results page offered a YouTube video titled 'Burning a Diamond in Liquid Oxygen,' which she selected, and Tasenetnethor gasped when John Thomas himself appeared on the computer screen.

She hadn't expected this. The video was of terrible quality, originally captured on Betamax tape and later digitized, but it was unmistakably him, stationed at the front of a large lecture hall, looking endearingly awkward in his cute suit and white lab coat. Tasenetnethor hadn't been the only entity in the room nurturing a crush that afternoon. But she'd had no idea that someone with a camera would be recording. That hadn't been so common a thing, a few decades back.

Seeing his image felt bittersweet. "Diamonds are nothing but carbon in crystalline form," he told his long-dismissed and now middle-aged students, as he poured a steaming draught of liquid oxygen from a double-walled flask into a glass beaker. He next picked up a small diamond with a pair of tongs (an unlovely hunk of industrial grade rock, a gem in chemical composition only) and held it under a gas torch flame. "Under the right conditions," he continued, waiting until the stone began to glow, "—that carbon can react with O_2 and become CO_2, carbon dioxide, the very air we exhale. The key is providing plenty of oxygen."

With that, Dr. Tinsdale dropped his hot rock into the beaker of cold blue fluid. It flared hot and white, blowing out the video image for a moment so that the rest of the lecture hall receded into dimness while the tiny diamond skittered and sizzled in the bottom of the laboratory glass. Finally it winked out and vanished in a puff of steam, like a magic trick or a movie mad scientist's best special effect.

The nearly-antique video ended with applause from the mesmerized students.

When it was over Cordelia Gray looked again at the Gemetic Memories product sitting up on her stepmother's bookshelf, and burst into tears.

Tasenetnethor saw Derren's shoulders stiffen, afraid that his girl might have been hurt by this experiment despite her assurances.

Nora hurried in from the back room, plopped down on the bed (after a fast assessment of the situation), and dragged the younger woman into her arms.

"Cordie, honey, it's okay, it's gonna be all right," she murmured, and for a moment this only made Cordelia cry harder. But Nora squeezed her tight, soothing her with a continued string of endearments, and after a minute or so she was able to collect herself. She sat back and wiped her eyes.

"I am so sorry. How embarrassing."

Nora dismissed the need for contrition with a slight shake of her head. "What were you looking at that got you so upset?"

"Oh, it's ridiculous. I mean... here, look." Cordelia turned the computer around and replayed the video. Tasenetnethor felt her chest grow tight, watching it again. She knew John Thomas was still alive and somewhat well, though she hadn't troubled him in more than twenty years. It only took one visitation by an actual spirit to undo decades of medication and therapy, which would be unconscionable, as it was her meddling that had occasioned his need for treatment in the first place. It may not have been possible for her to touch another ghost, but she could make herself plain to a living person in quite a number of ways, involving all five of the bodily senses. The wonders she'd worked with the young chemist's nervous system had been a source of mutual delight, for a time, but they'd also damaged his sense of reality, resulting in hospitalization, ignominy, and the ruin of his academic career. Today he worked for a swimming pool supply service, testing acidity levels in water samples and dispensing chlorine pellets by the pound. It may not have been the zenith of his potential, but it was a life. He had a girlfriend he lived with, a retired nurse, and he brewed craft beer in the garage of the house they rented together. Tasenetnethor would never let herself take those good, true things away from him, no matter how keen her longings became.

She realized from the ache in her jaw that she was gritting her teeth, while fighting back tears of her own. She was glad that Gray seemed unaware, focused as he was on his widow and youngest daughter.

The online chemistry demonstration ended for a second time.

Nora and Cordelia both looked over at the surplus medical oxygen reservoirs in the corner, then at each other.

"Do you think it would work?" Nora asked.

Cordelia shrugged. "The video didn't look fake. It was at UCLA. A long time ago, but it was in Young Hall. I recognize the classroom."

"What made you want to look that up?"

"I'm... not sure. I think I dreamed about it."

Nora got up and took the diamond from its box, holding the pendant up by the chain. Ptahshepses' artisans had curved a simple band of heavy silver into a teardrop-shaped cradle for the oversize stone. "It is beautiful, isn't it?"

Cordelia nodded. That much was hard to dispute.

"I have no idea what they meant, giving this to me, when they knew they were gonna kick up all this foolishness over the will. It feels like some symbolic message in a mafia movie, like a fish left on a doorstep or something. You know?"

"Like getting the Kiss of Death."

"Exactly. It seems almost, I don't know—malevolent, somehow. Being made from your father's ashes and all. Like it's part of some cruel joke I'm not in on."

Cordelia frowned. "Nora, this arbitration tomorrow? We don't have to. I mean, if you've had enough of the twins and want to let this go, I'd understand."

"And let them get their way, just because they're still angry with your father?" Nora smiled. "No. It was a comfort to him, to us both, knowing his money would do good in the world after he was gone. Their issues with him were legitimate, but I'm not about to let them crap all over that."

76

Cordelia laughed. "I can see why he loved you, Nora. I do too, you know."

Tasenetnethor could tell the older lady was moved, and that Derren Gray was humbled.

Nora leaned in and kissed Cordie's forehead.

"Let's go see if we can't vaporize this rock."

Eight

NORA PRIED THE DIAMOND from its setting with a pair of pliers and put it in her kiln, which she'd been test-firing that evening without anything in it, ensuring it would reach cone thirteen for an upcoming project—a temperature range in excess of two thousand degrees Fahrenheit. She insisted on safety goggles with heavy leather gloves and aprons for herself and Cordie both, supplies she had on hand for working around the kiln. She had some concern that the stone might explode in the heat, though its lab-grown flawlessness made that less likely than it might have been with a natural gem.

One of the O_2 reservoirs was empty, since oxygen evaporated fast, but the second had been delivered only two weeks prior, due to an ongoing billing mixup with the medical supply company Nora had contracted with to provide for Derren's palliative care. That tank felt heavy, and they could hear liquid slosh deep inside when they shook it.

Figuring out how to disengage the plastic cap that housed the copper coils which allowed the frigid fluid within to sublimate into a breathable gas took about half an hour, and contravened the express commands of several angry red warning labels. Oxygen in its liquid state was cryonically cold and would cause severe chemical burns if it came into contact with bare skin, so the women proceeded with the caution of bomb squad technicians. They let off the pressure and soon came down to a last connector they could unscrew for unfettered access to the contents of the tank's inner hull.

"Let's do it outside," Nora said. "By the pool. In case we need to kick it in or something."

Cordelia helped her lug the tank through her studio and out into the yard. The dark-bottomed swimming pool, lit from below, glowed in the diamond's same shade of deep, clear blue. Banana leaves cast broad shadows, obscuring corners and making the yard feel larger than it was.

Nora went back to the kitchen for a big Pyrex measuring cup that she placed at the edge of the concrete deck.

Cordelia unscrewed the valve from the top of the oxygen tank and set the mechanism aside. Nora helped her upend the reservoir (both of them wearing their leather gauntlets) to pour a rush of blue fluid up to the top of the graded cup. It bubbled madly, boiling off already into the cool spring air. The outside of the Pyrex glass whitened with an instant coat of frost.

"Nora, are you sure you want to do this? Rachel and Gwen did pay thirty grand for that diamond."

"And weren't they quick to let me know it?" Nora shook her head, opening the kiln door to reveal a searing hot stone inside. "Not my fault they never learned the value of a dollar. Do you want to do the honors?"

She offered Cordelia a pair of tongs and then stood back, brandishing a red fire extinguisher.

"This is it, Derren Gray. Be ready."

Gray's ghost looked a bit panicked, now that his expected eternity had come down to minutes, if not less. But he swallowed hard, and nodded. Tasenetnethor would have taken his hand if she could.

Cordelia gingerly picked up the red-hot rock with the tongs and carried it across the deck. She looked to Nora, aware that this was, in some sense, her father's final funeral. Nora nodded back, holding her fire extinguisher at the ready and looking resolute, though Tasenetnethor could see her eyes shining behind her plastic goggles.

There was nothing more that needed to be said.

When Cordelia dropped the superheated diamond into the hypercooled fluid, like some adventurous alchemist of old, the reaction was spectacular. Like the birth of a star in miniature, captured in a glass.

Nora yelped and Cordie leapt back from the instant, violent blaze of hot white light, too brilliant for them even to look at during the reaction's first few moments. Fresh CO_2 billowed into the night air as the bonding of oxygen and hot carbon continued at a vigorous rate. Dense, glowing steam over-spilled the Pyrex vessel and poured across the backyard deck in rolling tendrils, like billows of theatrical fog creeping across a stage. The burning gem rattled against the glass cup's walls, glaring like a tiny sun through a scrim of springtime haze.

Nora and Cordelia watched the light show at a safe distance, squeezing each other by the hand.

Derren Gray and Tasenetnethor watched from just behind them, so close and yet unknown.

"Thank you," he said to Tasenetnethor.

"Go to them," she suggested, tipping her head toward the women. "Last chance."

Derren took her advice, smiling and stepping forward to lay a hand on each of their shoulders a bare instant before the diamond expired, and the glass went dark.

The last gasp of his physical form joined the atmosphere like a final exhalation, and when the startled women whirled around, there was nobody behind them.

Nobody but Tasenetnethor, whom they couldn't see.

They missed the final pop of light, the last fizzle of oxygen in the bottom of the measuring cup. Only the old ghost saw Derren Gray vanish, like a diaphanous wisp of vapor in a breeze.

"Did you—?" Cordie ventured.

Nora nodded. "I felt it. A touch. Like a hand on my shoulder."

"Do you think...?"

Nora smiled. "Maybe, honey. Who can know, until we get there?"

Nine

CORDIE RE-CAPPED THE oxygen tank and Nora shut down her kiln before they went inside, to share a glass of wine before going to bed. They needed their rest, as they'd be facing down the twins' attorneys in the morning, in defense of Derren Gray's philanthropic legacy.

Tasenetnethor didn't follow them in. She wanted to be alone for a moment, with the cool chlorine smell of the lit-up pool and the soft rustle of banana leaves for comfort.

Christabel stepped out of the shadows. She'd been hovering for some time, to judge by her expression.

"Why?"

Because, fuck Ptahshepses. "It was what he wanted. It was only luck that I happened to know how to do it."

"From your chemist, was it? The one you sent mad?"

"Yes."

"I liked him," Christabel said, meaning Derren Gray and not John Thomas. "Not a lot of company for us, is there?"

"Should I have lied? Withheld what I knew, even when he told me his wishes? For the sake of having company?"

Christabel shrugged. Tasenetnethor didn't know that she felt much more certain about her choice, but it was too late for second thoughts.

"What's done is done," she said.

"Right. So it is." Christabel seemed about to say something more, scowling off across the pool, but then gave up on it with a shake of her head. "Be seein' you then, yeah?"

Tasenetnethor hoped so. It didn't feel certain. "For the solstice?"

Christabel gazed at her for a moment, rather critically, then was gone without answering, snapping back to Necromance.

Tasenetnethor sighed. She wasn't about to chase her back to the store. She wouldn't even know what she wanted to say. Not before she'd had some time to sort out her feelings.

Wraith Ladies Who Lunch

She'd just have to wait and see if Christabel turned up at the Cheesecake Factory in June.

Ten

SHE FELT TOO KEYED UP for repose, so she spent the remainder of the night touring her museum, visiting old favorite pieces like the sculpture of a petulant Satan cast in bronze by Jean-Jacques Feuchère, in Paris, right around the time she was being unearthed from her tomb outside of Thebes by a wonderstruck wandering Scotsman.

She found it hard to fathom that more than a hundred and seventy years could have already gone by since then.

Now that she knew, from Derren Gray's example, that it was still possible to go, she wondered how much time she might have yet to serve. She was bound by nothing more than painted paper cartonnage bundled around a collection of dry old bones—a move to a damp climate could ultimately do her in, if the rot the desert had put on hold were to recommence. Spongy old Britain had been a considerable risk to her existence, but Los Angeles felt drier and hotter every year.

She imagined she'd be staying for a while.

And she wondered what she might yet see come to pass. Everything Derren had elected to miss. Pharaohs and Caesars, Popes and Kings, now Prime Ministers and Presidents too—the self-important lot of them had already paraded by in the centuries since she perished. News of their reigns reached her like a sort of sociopolitical background noise, notable only in comparison to the shouts and bellows of those interchangeable barbarians who were always ready to stage a comeback. Eras when learning was held in low esteem were more deleterious than termites, to antiquities like her. Yet those ages when strength was prized for its own sake, and not for its power to preserve more fragile things, always came around again.

Not that civilization as it currently stood was ready to consign itself to the sands.

Maybe soon, but not tomorrow.

And that was good, because even after all this time, there were a couple books left in the world that she still wanted to read.

Back in her gallery, just before dawn, Tasenetnethor removed an old bronze sistrum from the display case across from her coffin and imagined it new, its metal beads ready to clash and jangle when shaken. But 'sistrum' was really a Roman word, a Latin word, applied by later conquerors. In her lifetime Tasenetnethor had known the instrument as a *sesheshet*, after the sibilant sound it made. She missed the rhythms of the temple rituals, and the perfume from the resinous incense cones the dancers wore, which warmed and melted with their exertions. She still remembered their steps, and tentatively tried them out, keeping time with her ankh-shaped noisemaker.

She took it up to the roof before she could start to feel foolish and stood facing east, looking toward the cantilevered top of the Pavilion for Japanese Art and the silent city that sprawled out beyond the museum grounds. The sky had brightened to a pale faience blue, though the sun had yet to clear the horizon.

She shook her sesheshet, recalling the music of the flutes and the cadence of the drums she'd once accompanied. She remembered the triumph and delight of those long-ago dawns when she, along with scores of other performers, had coaxed the sun back into the sky with the power of song. It felt good to remember that, and to recreate it, if only for her own amusement. She imagined a hundred other dancers shimmying with her, raising their voices to rekindle the day.

For the first time in a long time Tasenetnethor, the sistrum player of Amun-Re, found herself dancing alone to open the eye of morning.

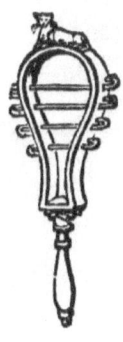

Epilogue

...One Week Later

"I CAN'T SEE YOU BUT I know you're there."

The priest's words made Tasenetnethor realize she'd forgotten what real alarm felt like.

She hovered in the Egyptian gallery's furthest corner, pressed up against the ceiling near the security camera and refusing to commit to a visible form, while Ptahshepses the Undying looked down on her mummy, secure in its plexiglass museum case.

She hoped it was secure, anyway. She really had no idea. The old sorcerer's abilities were beyond her capacity to gauge. Perhaps even to imagine. He looked the same as he had when she'd known him, some centuries before the ascendency of Rome. His Italian suit was a modern-day equivalent to the finery he'd enjoyed in Thebes, nearly three thousand years in their shared past. Neither his bald head nor his solemn and dangerous demeanor had ever changed, not in all that time. He retained (or affected) a hint of an accent—one that sounded like the result of upper-crust British schooling laid over the vestiges of some disused native tongue.

"What a remarkable thing it is to find you here," he said. "Imagine it, my own age-old work, displayed in the same institution as Rembrandt, Picasso, and so many other masters of their crafts. The only shame is that I remain uncredited amongst them."

His ego seemed as undiminished as his health.

"Show yourself, Tasenetnethor. I can compel you, but I would prefer to invite you."

Fuck that. If he could do it, he could prove it. Tasenetnethor stayed glued to the ceiling, invisible as the air. She wasn't about to do as he told her.

Ptahshepses' long face lengthened further, into a familiar scowl. His dark brows drew together like clouds massing on a far horizon, signaling the possibility of a storm.

A week had passed since Tasenetnethor's last lunch with Christabel, and Derren Gray's last day on earth. Right now, first thing on a slow weekday morning, she and Ptahshepses had her gallery all to themselves. Even the security guards were elsewhere, perhaps paid off or psychically deflected by Ptahshepses, so that he might talk to nobody without being taken for a schizophrenic.

"It was your friend Gray who alerted me to your presence here, so don't imagine you're hiding."

Maybe not, but he wasn't rushing to compel her into visible appearance either, she noticed. At least some of his threats were no more than hot air.

 But Derren...

How could Ptahshepses know what she'd done with Derren? Unless...

Tasenetnethor flickered into view, on the far side of her coffin, and Ptahshepses smiled. His grin had no mirth or warmth in it—only a sort of wicked satisfaction. The expression of a wolf baring its fangs in response to the scent of fear.

"What did you do to Derren?"

"Well, I had a second stone, you see," the tall man said, producing it from the pocket of his slacks. This gem was smaller by far than the monster purchased by Derren Gray's twins, but it had the same deep blue tint, like a clear sky at twilight. "A redundant safeguard, in case the primary anchor should ever become compromised. When his widow burned his daughters' very generous gift (at your instigation, I understand), Derren Gray was returned to me. And he told me all about you. You and Christabel. But don't blame him. He had absolutely no choice in the matter."

Ptahshepses drew Christabel's mourning pendant from inside his jacket.

"It took no more than the swipe of a credit card for me to re-acquire this," he said, considering the funereal charm he'd made for Harry Shelby more than a hundred and thirty years ago. "Nowhere near as elegant as my current work, yet still a monumental advance in technique when compared with something like you."

Tasenetnethor frowned, unsure of how affronted she should be by that remark. "Your sister murdered me," she said.

"Yes, she rather hated you, I'm afraid. All because of that scribbler with the paint-stained hands. What was his name again?"

"Amenemopet."

"Amenemopet, of course. I never understood what you ladies saw in him."

"You're the reason I'm still here." She meant this very much as an accusation.

Ptahshepses tipped his head, perhaps as the slightest of apologies. "Isetnofret asked it of me. She was wounded by her husband's betrayal, and humiliated by the gossip that ensued. And I wanted to see if it could be done, trapping a person between life and death."

"That's all? You wanted to see if you could?"

Ptahshepses shrugged. "You were something of a rough draft."

Tasenetnethor would have driven a knife through his chest, if she could. She might also have flown at him to see what havoc she might wreak with his nervous system if she really put her mind to it—to see if she might induce vertigo or terrifying hallucinations—but she found herself restrained from doing this as well. It was as if she had no volition, when she tried.

"I am protected by many wards," Ptahshepses explained, as though he knew exactly what she was considering. "You surely will appreciate my need for precaution."

Tasenetnethor appreciated that he'd have to be an idiot not to watch his ass. "What do you want?" she demanded, fighting to keep the quaver out of her voice. "Why are you here?"

"Those are the questions that have kept me alive. Many times I have thought I had answered them, and as often I have changed my mind."

He saw her looking at Christabel's pendant, which he still held in his hand like an offering.

"She is mine to control," he said. "To command to visible appearance or to send out as a spy to report on my enemies. Derren Gray as well. I could do as much with you... but for one thing."

"You'd need my artifact," Tasenetnethor said, in a flash of insight. "You never made a backup for me."

Ptahshepses nodded, awarding her points for cleverness. "Correct. You were my first effort, and I had not thought of it then. Today, an Egyptian mummy is not as easily purchased from a public museum as is a pendant from an antique store. A concerted exercise of wealth and influence might yet accomplish it, despite new laws restricting the trade in antiquities, but making so conspicuous a spectacle of my resources would hardly be more circumspect than performing my rituals right here in this gallery."

Did that mean she was... safe? Truly safe? Tasenetnethor couldn't believe it.

Ptahshepses smiled at her undisguised distrust. "I can of course exert my will while standing here over your corpse. My rites need only be enacted within my mind to be effective. But I can't stand here forever, can I?"

"Not without inviting attention."

"And attention is something I have long been wise to avoid."

Tasenetnethor nodded at Christabel's pendant. "Can I see her before you take her away? And Derren? Or is even that too much to ask?"

Her pride would never allow her to say 'please,' though her heart was nearly fluttering with anxiety over the thought of being left entirely alone again. She vibrated with the rage and frustration she normally did her best to deny, but which caused her to lash out now and then, like Christabel, and sometimes with more anger than she expected. Right now she wanted to shriek and hurl epithets if she couldn't throw fists, though such a display could only make this nightmare worse.

Ptahshepses regarded her with his heavy-lidded eyes. "Seeing you has reminded me of dawn over the river. Of the scent of lilies, and the pulse of drums. Sunsets over the necropolis of Khert-Neter. Do you recall these things as well?"

Tasenetnethor nodded.

"I had thought I was the last to remember. Isetnofret died a natural death, so long ago."

Wraith Ladies Who Lunch

Tasenetnethor couldn't conceal a smirk, despite her terror. Ptahshepses caught it, but sort of chuckled.

"She was my sister and I cared for her, but I would not have cared to share eternity with her. I know what she was like. Once I had a colleague, shall we say, who followed me across the years, but I've heard nothing of him for centuries, and in any case our relationship had... soured, long before. So I know what it is to stare into the maw of time with no companion at my side."

'Thom Shepcease' took a smartphone from his pocket and pretended to fumble it to the floor. He dropped to his knee to retrieve it, taking care to keep his back facing the security camera, and deftly drew off a strip of gray tape from a small roll he produced from somewhere inside his coat. He set Christabel's old hair pendant and Derren Gray's backup diamond onto the tape, then slapped it up under the table Tasenetnethor's coffin rested on as he stood and turned back to camera, displaying the dropped iPhone and appearing to inspect it for damage.

His performance was neat, quick, and convincing— worthy of a pickpocket or a prestidigitator.

"I have many ushabtis to serve me, and I can always make more," Ptahshepses said, angling his face away from the video lens before he spoke. "You have greater need of this pair than I, and I trust you will appreciate their company."

Was he serious? Tasenetnethor didn't know what to say. Conciliation was the last thing she expected from the long-lived priest. There had to be a catch.

"Perhaps I will come and speak with you in the tongue of our people, from time to time. If you would be amenable?"

Tasenetnethor nodded, and Ptahshepses tipped his head, then walked away.

The sistrum player's ghost slumped back against her body's plastic museum case. She couldn't catch her breath, though she had no need to breathe. Her legs wouldn't stop trembling.

Christabel walked into the gallery, tentatively, like she couldn't believe it either, from the direction of the porcelain and decorative arts collections. Derren Gray also entered, from the other side of the room, coming around the case that contained several small statues of Bastet and Horus. He too looked shaken, but otherwise undamaged.

Tasenetnethor had precious little idea of what she might have agreed to by accepting this favor—not that she'd been given any opportunity to refuse it. Not that she would have if she could have. But still. Being indebted to a creature like Ptahshepses upset her, to say the very least.

He seemed to be asking little enough in return for his generosity. The idea of doing him even the slightest of favors rankled, but she could imagine that the relentless flow of time might eventually blunt even Ptahshepses' roughest edges. He'd done exactly the last thing she might have expected.

Loneliness could effect the most unpredictable transmutations, she supposed.

"So was he for real, then, or what?" Christabel asked.

"I'm sorry," Derren Gray said, looking pained as he faced Tasenetnethor. "For telling him about you. I didn't mean to. I didn't want to."

"I know."

"Don't take it to heart," Christabel said. "I told him everything too. Was like I didn't have a choice, when he was holdin' that pendant."

"I'm sorry that burning your diamond didn't work the way we thought it would, Derren."

Gray nodded. It wasn't all right, precisely, but he was well aware that his situation could be much worse. It had been much worse, until a moment ago.

But now Ptahshepses was gone, on his way home to San Francisco.

Tasenetnethor crouched down to peer under her display table. The pair of lightweight relics were taped up there good, where no custodian was ever apt to spot them.

They might stay there for years. Or decades. That silver-gray duct tape was one of the modern world's enviable advances. She didn't doubt that Ptahshepses would have wrapped his mummies in it, had it been available during his natural lifetime.

So it looked like LACMA had a new pair of ghosts. And who knew how long they might be in residence? Even if someone discovered their anchoring artifacts they'd most probably be kept on-site, dropped in a storage drawer somewhere. So there was no point in worrying. Not on a bright spring morning, on a day made for feeling alive.

Tasenetnethor led her companions down to the open-air bar at the heart of the museum complex, where they could claim a corner table and pretend to have mimosas.

The End

Author's Note

Tasenetnethor really does reside at LACMA. If you visit, say hi for me.

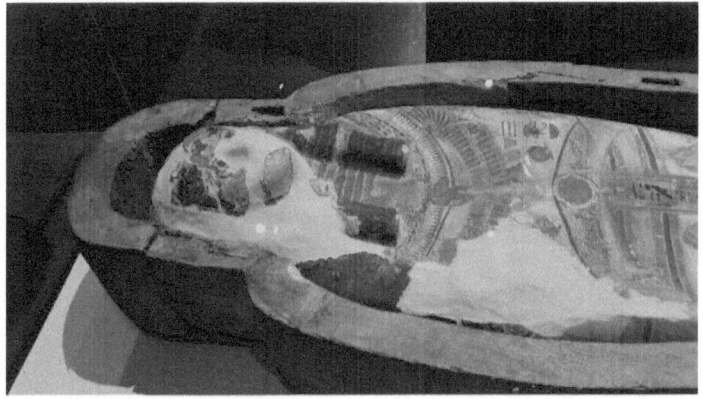

About the Author

Sean Patrick Traver is an LA native.
He's been visiting LACMA since the 1970s.

www.seanpatricktraver.com

www.ingramcontent.com/pod-product-compliance
Lightning Source LLC
Chambersburg PA
CBHW030558130626
46552CB00006B/2587

* 9 7 8 0 9 8 5 5 9 7 1 2 2 *